CHRISTOPHER MOORE read Modern Languages at New College, Oxford and also took a degree in Linguistics at the University of Edinburgh. He has worked as a journalist in London and Paris, taught in North Africa and the Middle East, written and edited a number of educational books for Heinemann and had three poetry anthologies published. His children's titles include *Peter William Butterblow* and *Wild Goose Lake* (both Floris Books). Christopher lives in Perth, Scotland.

CHRISTINA BALIT studied at Chelsea School of Art and the Royal College of Art. In 1982 she won a Thames Television Travelling Design Bursary and illustrated *Report to Greco* by Nikos Kazantsakis, then went on to illustrate *My Arabian Home* (Macdonald) and *The Oxford School Bible*. Titles for Frances Lincoln include *Blodin the Beast*, written by Michael Morpurgo, (shortlisted for the 1996 Kate Greenaway Medal), and *The Twelve Labours of Hercules*, written by James Riordan. Christina lives near Canterbury with her husband and two childr~

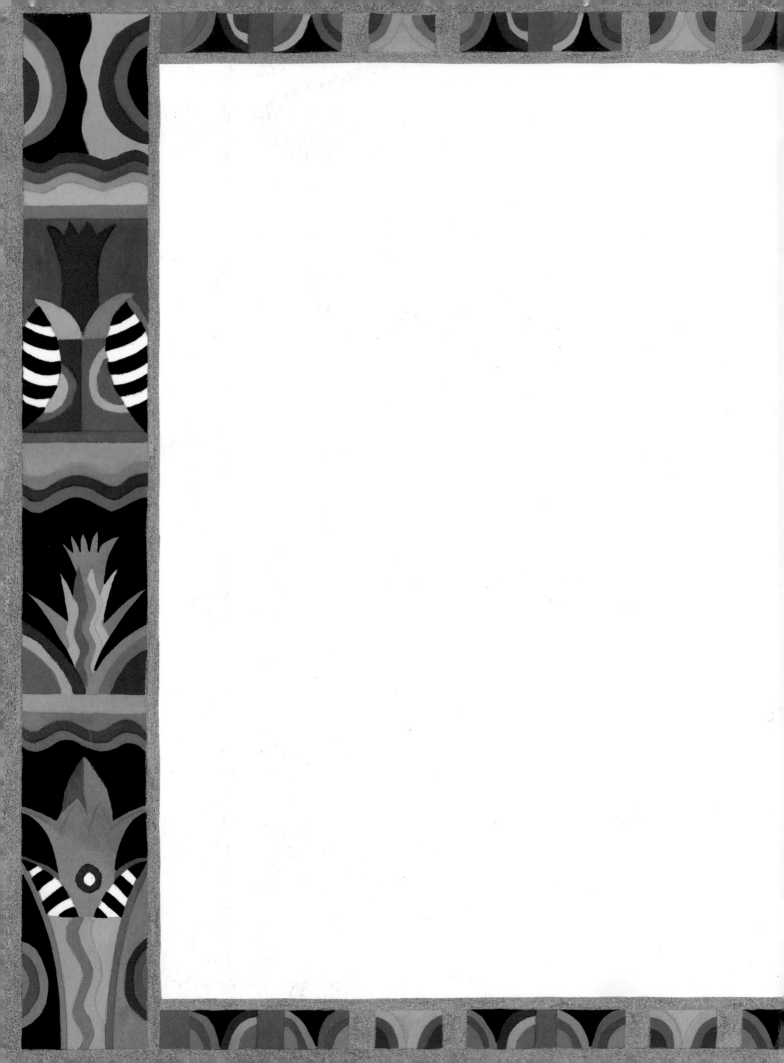

For Robyn – C.J.M.

For Sean-George, Billie-George and Crouch – C.B.

Ishtar and Tammuz copyright © Frances Lincoln Limited 1996
Text copyright © C.J. Moore 1996
The right of Christopher Moore to be identified as the author of this work
has been asserted by him in accordance with the Copyright, Designs
and Patents Act, 1988 (United Kingdom).
Illustrations copyright © Christina Balit 1996

First published in Great Britain in 1996 by
Frances Lincoln Limited, 4 Torriano Mews
Torriano Avenue, London NW5 2RZ

First paperback edition 1997

British Library Cataloguing in Publication Data
available on request

ISBN 0-7112-1090-X hardback
ISBN 0-7112-1099-3 paperback

Set in 16/20pt AGaramond

Printed in Hong Kong
1 3 5 7 9 8 6 4 2

ISHTAR
AND TAMMUZ

A Babylonian Myth of the Seasons

Adapted and retold by Christopher Moore

Illustrated by Christina Balit

FRANCES LINCOLN

In long ago Babylon, four thousand years past, Ishtar was worshipped as queen of the stars and goddess of all creation. No being was more beautiful, more powerful or more terrible. By day, she spread her blue-lined robe over the world which she had helped the gods to create. By night, as Venus and moon-goddess,

she drove her chariot of bright silver among the stars.

Ishtar held the power of life and death over all. Sometimes she brought storms, hail and thunder down upon the earth. Sometimes in her darker moods she brought down the terror and destruction of war.

Ishtar loved the earth so much that one day she sent her son, Tammuz, to live there.

Wherever he walked, the earth brought forth fruit and crops and the green of the land. The birds and animals followed the sound of his flute for sheer joy, and the people welcomed him and loved him dearly. They called him the Green One.

From the heavens above, Ishtar watched her son and was content.

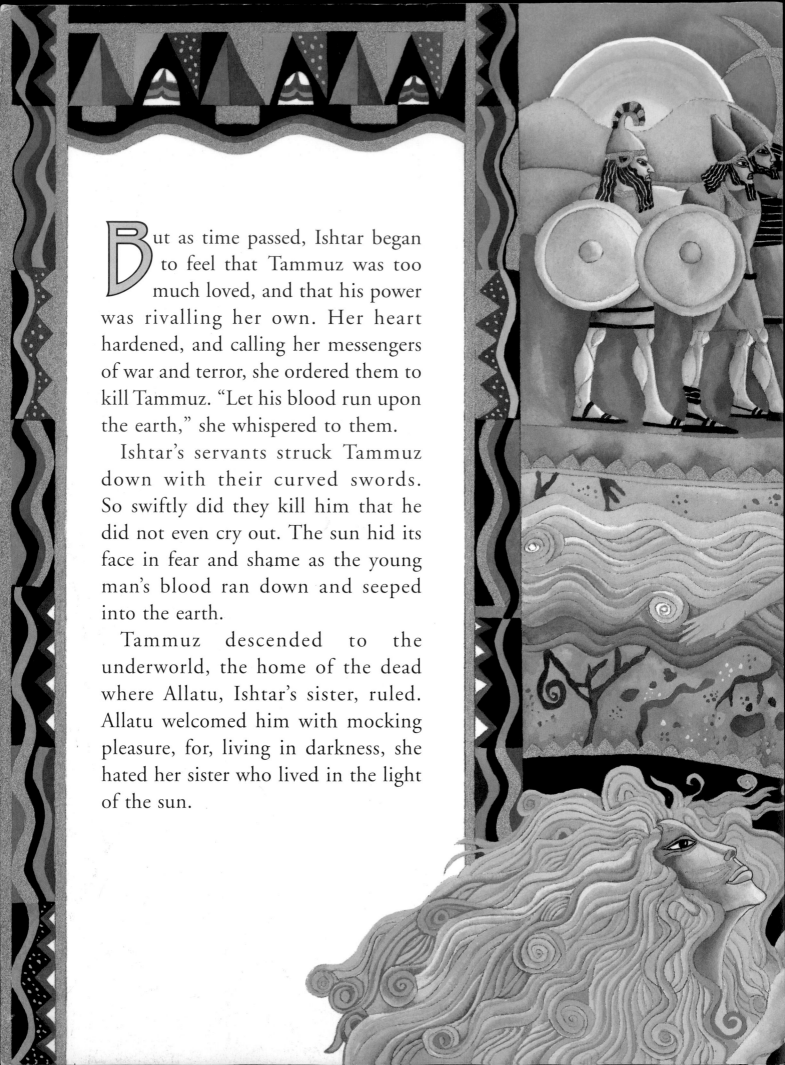

But as time passed, Ishtar began to feel that Tammuz was too much loved, and that his power was rivalling her own. Her heart hardened, and calling her messengers of war and terror, she ordered them to kill Tammuz. "Let his blood run upon the earth," she whispered to them.

Ishtar's servants struck Tammuz down with their curved swords. So swiftly did they kill him that he did not even cry out. The sun hid its face in fear and shame as the young man's blood ran down and seeped into the earth.

Tammuz descended to the underworld, the home of the dead where Allatu, Ishtar's sister, ruled. Allatu welcomed him with mocking pleasure, for, living in darkness, she hated her sister who lived in the light of the sun.

On the upper earth, after the death of Tammuz, all growing things withered and died. The crops and grasses shrivelled, leaves curled and fell. The birds fell silent, nothing bloomed and the earth grew barren.

With Tammuz gone, a dull sadness came upon the world.

At first, the people felt only the loss of a loved one. But as the rivers and springs ran dry, hunger and thirst followed. The beasts of the field could not survive for long on the parched earth. The unhappy people cried out to Ishtar and, as each day passed, their prayers grew more desperate.

Finally, Ishtar heard their prayers. When she came down to the earth she had helped to create, she found an all but lifeless place with trees bare, meadows without grass or flowers, the birds huddled and silent. The very ground seemed hard as stone, chill as winter. She saw the faces of the people sad and tired and heard their laments. She saw their offerings upon the altar, the clouds of incense and the uplifted arms of the priestess.

"Ishtar, Queen of Heaven," cried the priestess, "take our precious seed corn, take the last fruits of our orchards. Be merciful and let Tammuz walk again among us. He is the green spirit of the land, the source of breath and birth." The priestess set fire to the offerings and the smoke rose into the sky.

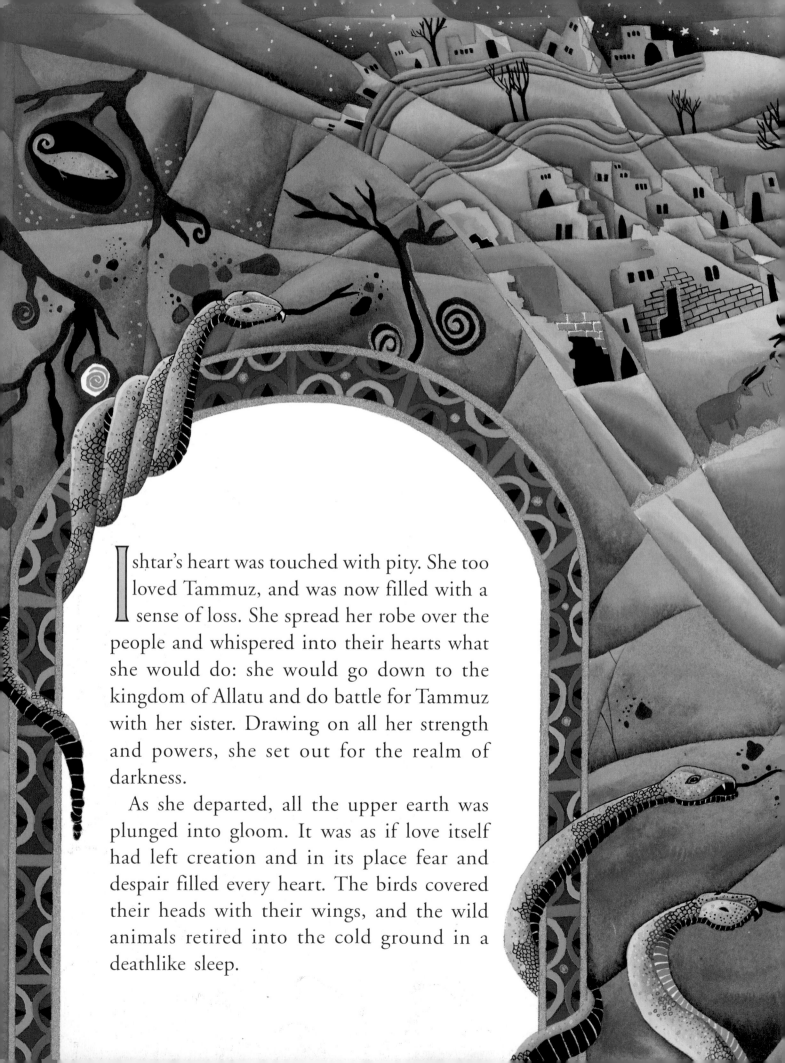

Ishtar's heart was touched with pity. She too loved Tammuz, and was now filled with a sense of loss. She spread her robe over the people and whispered into their hearts what she would do: she would go down to the kingdom of Allatu and do battle for Tammuz with her sister. Drawing on all her strength and powers, she set out for the realm of darkness.

As she departed, all the upper earth was plunged into gloom. It was as if love itself had left creation and in its place fear and despair filled every heart. The birds covered their heads with their wings, and the wild animals retired into the cold ground in a deathlike sleep.

Ishtar entered the dark cavern which led to the world below. Down and down she went, until at last she came to the cold grim city of the dead with its seven walls and seven gates, where her sister ruled.

At the sight of this forbidding place, her courage almost failed her. No living thing, she knew, had ever returned from Allatu's realm. But she thought of Tammuz, and was filled with the strength of her love for him.

At the first gate, she called out to the watchman, "I am Ishtar, queen and goddess. Open so that I may pass!"

The watchman replied, "Give up your crown and you may pass. It is Allatu's command." Ishtar, furious, had no choice but to obey.

At the second gate, she was made to surrender the necklace of beads at her throat, the symbol of her power over the night heavens.

At the third gate, she had to give up her pendant earrings. But she thought still of Tammuz, and went on.

When she came to the fourth gate, Ishtar's bracelets of gold were taken from her wrists and ankles.
At the fifth gate, she had to give up the jewels from her breast.
At the sixth gate, she put off her girdle of birthstones.
At the seventh and last gate, she had to leave her silken gown.

As she passed through the gates, one by one, she heard each grim
door being shut and bolted behind her.

So, stripped of all her royal splendour and powers, Ishtar entered
the very heart of the citadel.

llatu, goddess of the underworld, half-woman, half-lioness, sat upon her jewelled throne surrounded by snakes and salamanders.

She laughed triumphantly to see Ishtar come defenceless before her. Beside the throne, Tammuz sat as if half-asleep. He did not stir or even seem to recognise his mother.

Ishtar stood before the dreadful figure and bowed her head. Then she fell on her knees and pleaded with her sister: to humble herself was her only hope – she had no powers left to do battle. But Allatu only laughed at her.

"Let me at least touch my beloved son," cried Ishtar.

"No!" screamed Allatu in fury – but too late, for Ishtar had leapt past the guardians of the throne to the side of Tammuz, and was embracing her son, the tears streaming from her eyes.

Bathed in Ishtar's warm tears, Tammuz felt the waters of life touching him once more. He awoke, and clung to his mother so closely that Allatu's guards could not separate them.

"Take him!" cried Allatu bitterly. "But do not think you have overcome my powers. You may both leave my realm – on one condition: Tammuz must return to me for six months every year."

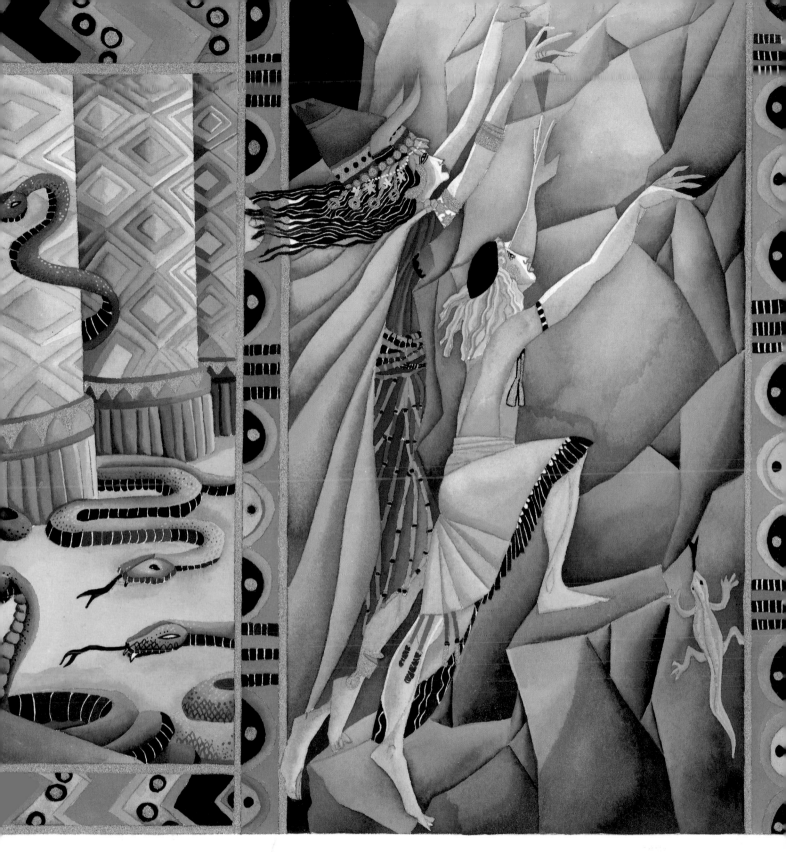

Ishtar and Tammuz had to agree. Together, they hurried back through the seven great gates. One by one, Ishtar's queenly gown, girdle, bracelets and jewels were restored to her until she stood, crowned once more, outside the realm of the dead. Then mother and son climbed through the dark caverns towards the upper earth.

When Tammuz stepped out on to the earth above, he kissed the ground for joy. Warmth and new life poured into all creation, song rose in the throats of the birds, and the animals broke from their deep sleep.

From this time on, so it would be each year. When Tammuz was summoned back to the underworld, cold winter descended on the land for six months.

But with his return each spring, nature woke again with joy, the trees felt the pulse of new sap and every seed in the ground stirred. Among the people a new liveliness was born. Dance and music filled the houses, and in every farm, village, town and city, thankful prayers were offered for the return of Ishtar's beloved son, Tammuz.

A Note from the Author

To the people of ancient Mesopotamia (now Syria and Iraq) who grew crops and grazed their herds on the fertile plains of the rivers Tigris and Euphrates, the goodwill and the blessings of the earth-goddess Ishtar were all-important.

Ishtar loved the semi-divine shepherd-king Tammuz. Early myths say their marriage ensured that the earth remained fruitful, but the great epic of Gilgamesh tells how Ishtar's power destroyed Tammuz. In one version of the story, Ishtar descended to the Underworld to find him, and was allowed to return from the Underworld so long as Tammuz spent half the year there in her place.

For this simplified retelling I have made Tammuz the son of Ishtar, as he is often called 'my son' in the ancient laments of Ishtar. The name Tammuz comes from an earlier form, Dumuzi, meaning 'faithful son'.

A similar mythical account of nature's yearly cycle – summer harvest followed by barren winter – can be found in the more familiar Greek myth of Demeter and Persephone. But this earlier story of Ishtar and her beloved Tammuz, with its origins some 5,000 years before Christ, also has much to teach us about cherishing the earth and harvesting it with care.

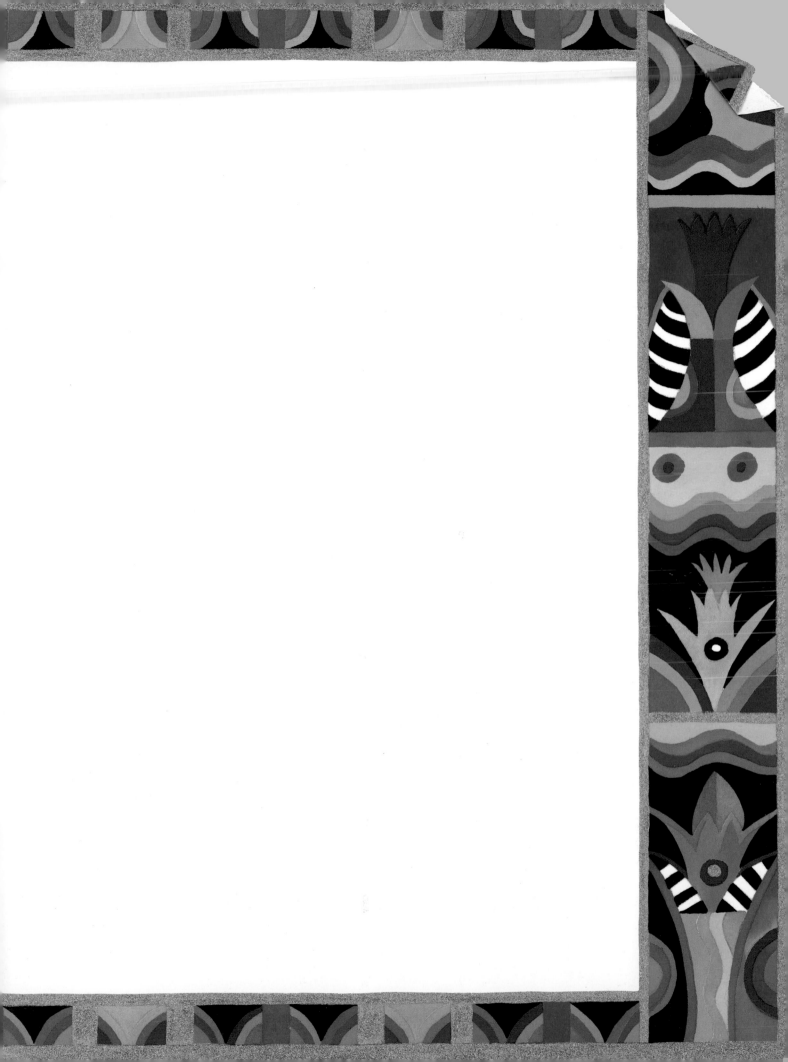

OTHER PICTURE BOOKS IN PAPERBACK FROM FRANCES LINCOLN

BLODIN THE BEAST
Michael Morpurgo
Illustrated by Christina Balit

Blodin the beast stalks the land, breathing fire and razing villages to ruins. Only wise old Shanga, weaving his magic carpet, knows how to destroy the monster, but he is too old to cross the mountains that never end. A timeless tale of a young boy's quest to save his people that will enchant children of every age.

Suitable for National Curriculum English - Reading, Key Stage 2
Scottish Guidelines English Language - Reading, Level C

ISBN 0-7112-0910-3   £4.99

PEPI AND THE SECRET NAMES
Jill Paton Walsh
Illustrated by Fiona French

When his father is commanded to decorate Prince Dhutmose's tomb, brave Pepi, armed only with his quick wits and a knowledge of secret names, sets out to bring back real-life models of the terrifying animal gods for his father to paint. A thrilling story that brings alive the magic of ancient Egypt.

Suitable for National Curriculum English - Reading, Key Stage 2; History, Key Stage 2
Scottish Guidelines English Language - Reading, Levels C and D; Environmental Studies, Levels C and D

ISBN 0-7112-1089-6   £5.99

LITTLE INCHKIN
Fiona French

Little Inchkin is only as big as a lotus flower, but he has the courage of a Samurai warrior. How he proves his valour, wins the hand of a princess, and is granted his dearest wish by the Lord Buddha is charmingly retold in this Tom Thumb legend of old Japan.

Suitable for National Curriculum English - Reading, Key Stages 1 and 2
Scottish Guidelines, English Language - Reading, Levels A and B

ISBN 0-7112-0917-0   £4.99

Frances Lincoln titles are available from all good bookshops.
Prices are correct at time of publication, but may be subject to change.